I0779080

Boxed In

And

Other Stories

Boxed In
And Other Stories

Andrew Kim

The Hermit Kingdom Press
Highland Park * Seoul * Bangalore * Cebu

Paperback ISBN13: 978-1-59689-112-8

Write To Address:
The Hermit Kingdom Press
P. O. Box 1226
Highland Park, NJ 08904-1226
The United States of America

Library of Congress Cataloging-in-Publication Data

Kim, Andrew.
  Boxed in and other stories / Andrew Kim.
      p. cm.
  ISBN 978-1-59689-112-8 (hardcover : alk. paper)
  I. Title.
  PS3611.I45285B69 2011
  813'.6--dc22
                            2011042753

Contents

"Boxed In"

The world is always so gray.

Looking out at the aggregating clouds, I couldn't help but feel suffocated in the classroom. The teacher was showily reciting pointless lines in Latin from plays I'd never heard of, trying to impress us with his college education as usual. He always rambled on about useless things that were neither interesting nor relevant to my life.

But then, nothing in school was really relevant to me, now was it?

The teacher's rant on the upcoming final exams was cut off by the bell, the signal for freedom seeming especially promising this day. Students around me stood up eagerly and chatted with each other excitedly about their plans for the rest of the day.

I, too, was itching to leave this hellhole of tests and textbooks. This was where I had no future; this was where I could do nothing but resign myself to fate.

I packed my notebook and pencil anxiously and stood up with more vigor than I usually showed in school. My strides was especially rushed today and only picked up speed once the winter winds bombarded me outside.

Once I was a good distance from the school gates, I paused to look up at the harbingers of rain. Actually, considering the temperature, snow was not an impossibility. Even the water that fell from the skies were gifted with an uncertain future, a fate not yet set in stone.

An especially gelid wisp of air made my body tense and shudder. I threw up the hood on my jacket and resumed the journey home.

With so much physical action to be done and my mind left free, my thoughts wandered. Final exams were very close; I only had two weeks to pointlessly worry about them before peacefully resigning to the destiny that I'd been given at birth. I hated the days before important tests with a very real passion because they only mocked me with the fancy of success when in reality I'd failed before I even took the test.

I sighed, mentally scolding myself for dwelling on facts I already knew, and decided to keep my mind off of my "fate." Two weeks was more than enough time for me to worry about my inevitable results.

Off the side of a run-down road that rarely saw vehicles of any kind was a path less traveled, barred off by a metal bar at abdomen-height with decaying yellow paint that no longer looked yellow. The sign attached to the middle of it, equally weathered by time, read "DO NOT ENTER. TRESPASSERS ARE PUNISHABLE BY LAW" in bold, once-red lettering. Now it was merely a friendly pink that failed to intimidate the pigeons that had broken up the peach-colored border of the sign with splatters of white. Using my hand to help hoist my body into the air, I hopped over the cold bar and walked on.

The weather matched the worn ruins of the district. Run-down remnants of what were once bustling shops, houses, and businesses now stood crippled by webbing crevices and green patches of algae and fungi. Grass left alone for many years too long boasted atrocious lengths in messy fields. It bent and swayed with the occasional breeze, forbidden from standing tall by the harsh environment.

Once, this was a refuge for people without government-given names. Ever since the implementation of the Chosen Future Program, newborns have been receiving their names from the government. Officially, this was supposed to somehow help organize the census, but it was actually just a way to force "fates" onto infants so that the government could choose who will be the foolish peasant and who will be the rich businessman. The process was "fair and unprejudiced," but politics never really works out that way. Naturally, there were parents who didn't want their children to be given names and fates from the government, and they gathered in havens such as this where they could name their own children. Ten years ago, though, the government cracked down on the rebellious groups and such shelters were eliminated. All that remained of this one? Unattended roads and broken buildings that kids occasionally played in as a test of courage or used as a shortcut home.

Below my feet, the road was filled with deep potholes and cracks accumulated over the years. Over the two years I have been taking this path to and from school each weekday, I have gotten injured many times by my own carelessness. With every month there was a new hole, a new fissure to break my leg over. And yet, somehow, this place had become my second home. Perhaps it was because I felt like I could empathize this deserted, hopeless land, or maybe it was because I could be my own depressed mess here without fearing discovery by some unwanted outside party. As honest and hardworking as my parents were, there were times when I preferred solitude over care.

Unexpectedly, I spotted an unwanted outside party in the distance, an unfamiliar *something* that seemed to be sprawled on grass off the side of the road. As I got closer, I began to make out some details. Arms that appeared to be so fragile that a strong wind would break them lied out, one straight and the other bent at an obtuse angle. Long hair fell from a small, thin frame. The strands seemed to be a brown color, but that could have been because of the splotches of dirt. From below the hair stuck out two famished legs caked with mud.

My mind took a few moments to process what my eyes were seeing, and in the meantime my legs took me closer. Once I was standing right above the petite body, I stooped to one knee and reached out a tremulous hand, unsure if I wanted to overturn this particular mystery. What if this was a fugitive killer? What if this was the corpse of a victim of a fugitive killer? What if this was a runaway kid with rabies?

After entire minutes of such ludicrous pondering, I finally decided that, whatever happened, it couldn't possibly make me a greater slave to my man-given fate. I placed a hand on a leg and a hand on an arm and flinched at how cold the skin was. Maybe this really was a corpse? Regardless, I felt as if I *had* to know why this body was here, so I turned it onto its back.

The first thing that I noticed was that chest was moving steadily up and down, bringing me much relief. Then I looked at the face and saw the young, muddy face of a girl. Aside from some flickering movement of her eyes that seemed to be reactions to my touch, her countenance reflected no anxiety or discomfort; she seemed to be sleeping perfectly fine in the below-freezing temperature with nothing more than a dirty, stained rag to ward off the cold.

I had company in this place for the first time since I began regularly walking across this district, and the visitor was an unconscious little girl who appeared to be homeless.

But now I squatted there, not sure what to do next. She might freeze to death if she just slept outside in the winter. On the other hand, maybe it would be a better idea to just mind my own business and pretend I never saw her. However, I'd definitely feel guilty about leaving a girl out sleeping in the freezing cold.

My mind worked frantically on finding a good excuse for leaving her alone. Maybe she was really a criminal and would assault me if I woke her up? Then I would be ashamed of lacking the confidence to fight off a starved girl, however insane she may be. Maybe she wanted to sleep out in the cold because she finds it relaxing? That made little to no sense. I might not even be able to help if I tried to get involved. But surely even a failure such as I can wake a girl up and give her some food or something. Eventually, I gave up; either I would move on and feel like a disgraceful wretch of a human being, or I would do something to help her out.

Irresolutely, I reached out and poked the girl in the arm. No reaction. Well, considering that she didn't wake up from getting rolled over, it only made sense that a poke would not be enough. Yet, I was uncomfortable with the thought of using any show of force to wake her up. I poked once more with a little more pressure, but still got no reaction. At this point, I decided to drop the meekness in my efforts and, laying her head on my knee to ensure that her head didn't hit solid ground, shook her shoulders with sizable vigor. She still didn't stir. I tried a number of methods that couldn't seriously harm her – tickling her feet, lightly tapping on her forehead, and so on. Somehow, she slept through every single one. It seemed as though, despite the uncomfortable conditions, the girl was sleeping just fine.

At last I capitulated to the endurance of her slumber. Now that I had put forth a legitimate attempt at waking her up and that has proven useless, I was free to go. I had given it my all, and in the end I wasn't able to help. The end.

Nagging in the back of my head, though, was the honest voice of my conscience: "No, you haven't. You haven't given it anything close to your all."

I was fed up with this stupid, annoying baggage called "guilt." Deciding that it would be of no serious consequence, I awkwardly scooped the girl up in my arms and walked down the road. The girl felt as though she were no heavier than my backpack.

In minutes, I was inside of a structure that was stable enough to stay in. Of all the buildings in this district, this was the one that was most favored by nature. Standing at a height of two stories, the bland concrete building was practically free of blemishes aside from the occasional crack or hole. In fact, it probably could have passed as just another boring structure that was never painted or decorated in an active city today. I'm not an expert in earth science, so I don't know exactly why this building suffered so little during the decade it was left alone, but the fact is that it was a building that could stand without a risk of collapsing at any moment, and that was all that mattered to me.

The entire bottom floor was one wide, tall room with few furnishings. Gray light leaked in through some large, noticeably clean windows, matching the stark concrete walls. Even after using this building as a fortress in times of bad weather for two years, I still wasn't entirely sure as to what this building was supposed to be used for. Rather than blaming my lacking deductive abilities, I point to the lack of remaining evidence as the cause. Over time, as animals wandered in and out and the weather worked on the building however it wanted, most furnishings were probably removed or destroyed. All that were left were a badly wrecked couch that couldn't be used for anything other than cruel and unusual punishment, a pile of gashed wood that may or may not have been a bunch of chairs at one point, and a pile of broken glass left to collect dust in a remote corner.

Unfortunately, there was nothing that I could really sit on. After a certain experiment involving a cheap three-legged stool and a mystery bestial thief, I'd decided against bringing any sort of furniture to this place. The bare floor proving too cold for comfort, I opted to remain standing, a little cold because I was short a layer.

My jacket was laid on the floor in order to protect the girl from the freezing floor that I myself was unwilling to touch. The contents of my backpack had been emptied out near a wall, allowing the shriveled skin of it to serve as a comfortable barrier between the girl's bare legs and the cold concrete.

The only article of clothing that this girl wore was a bland, large shirt marred brown and black by visiting unsavory locations. While the bottom of the shirt went down halfway down the girl's thighs, the sleeves were torn down to barely covering half of her upper arm. As far as I could tell, she was a homeless girl in poverty. Would she just go on her way after she woke up? Would I let her?

Well, I'd really have no other choice. I was in no position to take responsibility for another life. I was still a student, and my family lacked the financial security to afford another plate. Even if I wanted to make something out of this encounter, I was limited by practicality.

But I was getting ahead of myself. Did I really think that there was ever a chance of something happening? Day in and day out, people pray for extraordinary things to happen to them, and these unreasonable desires draw them into delusions of possibilities where objective probability clearly says that it isn't going to happen. It is a difficult and rare thing – breaking out of one's shell, that is. And sometimes, it's not your fault; sometimes, circumstances just tie you hand and foot.

I lifted my head at a mumble. The girl was beginning to shiver violently. She turned onto her stomach, still shaking, and weakly opened her eyes – straight at me. I gulped nervously. Naturally, she would suspect that I was some sort of pedophile kidnapper who stole her off the streets in order to get ransom out of her parents. Now she would run or lash out for her dear life, hopefully the former and the not the latter.

But I was wrong. This girl just stared at me, and I was stuck returning the favor. Her large eyes were a strange, bright gold, pure of any grudges or frustration. It was as if I was staring into the eyes of a newborn, completely oblivious as to what fate was in store for her.

It took surprisingly little time for the low temperatures to take a higher priority than my presence. The girl curled up on her knees, trembling again. I imagined what it would be like to be in her position, with barely any clothes in this already frigid weather. People complain all the time of being too cold on days such as this from the insulated environments of their own homes, so I can only imagine that most people would go nuts in my visitor's position. Yet, all she did was sit there and shake from the cold. Her breath did not seem to be helping the color of her hands much. I was unsure how I should go about dealing with this. My jacket, which was protecting her from the cold floor, wasn't being much use against the cold air, and my sweater – well, my sweater was for me. I mean, all I had underneath my sweater was a T-shirt, and we all know how unhealthy it is to be out in the cold in nothing but a... I looked at my visitor's bare arms and legs, squeezed against each other to maximize use of their body heat.

I hesitantly took my sweater by the hood and pulled it over my head, raising my shirt and letting it fall once the grip of friction let it go. The punch of the cold air went straight through my pathetic no-brand shirt and I think I had a good first-hand experience of what the girl was feeling. Well, I still had my pants, but I wasn't going to give her my pants, too.

Even though the girl didn't seem to have any vicious attacks in store for me at the moment, I still wanted to take caution. I threw my heavy sweater towards her; when it landed on the concrete, the sweater's gray matched perfectly.

The rustling of cloth piqued the kid's interest and she looked up. Her eyes rested on the sweater, wide open with some surprise, and then looked up at me. I just looked back, neither telling her to take it nor forbidding her from doing so. She took it eagerly and wrapped it around herself as if it were a blanket. Although the girl's application of the sweater was unorthodox, the immediate effect was obvious; the girl's shivers were reduced to barely being noticeable and her countenance calmed down a great deal. With the threat of the cold now gone, she turned her attention to me. Rather, she turned her stare towards me. Again with those unnaturally golden eyes...

She didn't seem to intend to initiate a conversation within the next hour, so I broke tradition and made the first move. "Who are you?"

A simple question, you'd think, but one made unnecessarily complex by the innumerable labels that people love to slap onto others. Identity crises are not all that uncommon at my age. Of all my identities, I have a default answer to the question "Who are you?" and that is-

"I don't know." The girl's voice was soft and sheepish, as if she was embarrassed.

I inquired further about what she meant by that. "I..." She hesitated, glancing at me furtively. She seemed to fear that I would do something bad to her if she told me. Even if she had her own issues, though, I still needed to know exactly what was going on in order to choose how to proceed. I opened my mouth to speak.

Suddenly, a low, squirming noise caught my attention. It took me a moment to identify a stomach's cry

for help. The girl's rosy face and embarrassed frown confirmed my suspicions.

I found myself smiling a little as I reached down to retrieve a couple of granola bars that I had left over from my snacks. I always brought more than I would eat in school just in case I wanted to hang out in this district a little longer.

The girl followed the colorful wrappers with a hungry eye, almost as if she was trying to see the edibles inside and eat them with her mind. This time, I approached her and handed her the gifts myself. She looked at the bars with some surprise before proceeding to loudly tear the wrappers apart and devouring the light snacks. I backed away towards the wall and watched her spend no more than fifteen seconds per bar. It made me wonder how long it had been since she had last eaten.

Once she was done licking off her fingers, the girl sat there pensively for a few moments with wrappers scattered all around her. She looked up at me with her innocent eyes, eyebrows slanted in contemplation, before she finally took a deep breath and spoke.

"I woke up a few days ago in the middle of a nearby forest. I didn't remember anything, but I was there. Without any memories of the past, I didn't know what to do, so I wandered around, looking for people. I saw some concrete buildings and ran towards them, leading me to this area. I figured that if I followed the road, I would get to where other people are, but then I was really tired, and..."

"And so you ended up fainting on the side of the road."

"Yes..."

A case of amnesia, huh. How surreal. I'd seen movies and TV shows with amnesiac characters. They were often important or dangerous people before their memory losses. I supposed that this wouldn't be the case with the girl, but I still felt odd seeing an amnesiac in person. Amnesia is just one of those things that you hear a lot about but you rarely actually come in contact with.

Of course, there was the possibility that she was just pulling my leg, but I didn't really see why she would lie to me. She definitely looked homeless, and she was sleeping outside in the middle of winter, so I was pretty sure that she actually had issues going on. Well, the details didn't really matter, anyway. Although...

"Do you really not remember anything?" I asked. "Not even your name?"

She shook her head, and I suddenly felt a mix of pity and jealousy – pity, for she knew nothing about herself and where she came from; jealousy, for she was not bound to a name of fate, for she had a blank slate to work with.

But now I had no idea what to do with this girl. She was an amnesiac, so she had nowhere to go. What was I supposed to do? It felt as if the cold was freezing my mental faculties and rendering me helpless. I could leave her alone. I should leave her alone. I knew nothing about her, and I couldn't take her home. Surely, she would be able to manage somehow. I gave her food, shelter, and some clothes. That should be enough. I'd already done my good deed.

I observed the girl with what I hoped was a poker face. She was nestling with the sweater and stealing quick glances at me, no doubt curious as to what I would do next. Really, she was the one who should have been more frightened, but somehow, I think that I was – frightened not of any immediate danger, but of my responsibilities as a human being.

"Are you the one who brought me here?" the girl suddenly asked with a brave face and a quivering voice. The silence must have been too much for her to bear.

Her unexpected question startled me a little bit, and all I could do was answer with an "Oh, yeah." How uncool.

As she was looking down at the floor, the girl mumbled something, but I couldn't hear, so I walked a little closer. "What was that?"

"Thank you," she stammered loudly, still keeping her eyes occupied with the dull ground. What, she was still just a kid after all. Honestly, I wished she hadn't said that. Once a girl thanks you like that, complete with the shy demeanor, it's a lot harder to just abandon her to the wilderness.

I watched her, sitting on the ground and shaking a little again. I was feeling enough like a jackass already, so I gave her a "You're welcome." But not really. I'd rather not be put in such a situation again.

But I didn't see it coming. She lifted her head towards me with lit-up eyes and a wide smile that would melt a thug's heart. As cold as she must have been, her countenance seemed to me a radiant, golden sun, however cliché that may sound. Somehow, she reminded me of my sister when she was younger.

Kids are hard to understand. They trust easily and lack the knowledge to fear what should be feared. A child believes that the only destiny that she could possibly have is one that is bright and hopeful. Her ignorance is her bliss, but also her greatest strength.

"Ah." The girl pointed out the large window behind me, and I turned. White drops danced down from the sky like angels descending to bless the land. Seeing them made me feel colder, and I shivered.

Looking back at the girl, I was surprised to see the look of wonder on her face. She opened her eyes wide and forgot to close her hanging mouth. I smiled. Only a child could be freezing and still take delight at the sight of snow.

Again I turned to look out at the snow through the window. Each flake had been given a beautiful fate. But at one point, surely each flake had been a droplet in the sea, or a dreary raindrop over an industrial city. Each fate is made up of many smaller "fates," just like how one person's identity is actually a conglomerate of many different "identities." Even if I had been given a fate from the government, there were plenty of things outside of what I knew to be my fate that I still governed. For example, I could leave this girl alone or I could try to help her begin a new story on her blank slate.

Somewhere along the course of my internal ramblings, I'd turned my head to look at my visitor, and now I noticed that she was staring back at me curiously. I gave her a smile, and she smiled back.

Maybe this encounter was a component of my fate. Maybe this girl was meant to add another color to my life. Or maybe circumstances would smack me in the face and I would never see this girl ever again. I didn't know the future. But I could at least make an effort to find out.

If she was meant to change my life, then I would give her time to change my life, and a couple years from now, perhaps I will be glad that I challenged the boxed-in "fate" that I had given myself.

"Distraction"

Click. Click. Click. Click.

Seated on a swerving chair was a fidgety young man staring at the lined paper waiting in front of him on a wooden desk as a sleeping patient awaits the scalpel. The doctor's thumb pushed down on the butt of his scalpel again and again, pumping out and retracting the tool's metal tip to the beat pulsating in his imagination. The only words he had written down so far comprised the title: "How I Make a Difference."

Next to his paper lied his cell phone, a free phone with a basic number pad and three navigation buttons, which he punched with his finger to conjure the time –

August 20, 5:09 PM. He leaned back and swerved his chair away from his opponent. Perhaps a little break would help clear his head and give him ideas later.

His eyes wandered aimlessly. He had made the decision to take a break - fantastic. But what would he do in that break? He had lost his DS at some unknown point during the week prior, and he was not in a mood to play an old game on his console. There seemed to be few methods for him to waste his time.

In the midst of his troubles, the teenager's eyes settled on a black spot on his white wall. How odd; this mark was not one that he recognized. It was small and round, distinguishing it from the seventeen black lines that he had accidentally drawn on his walls by means of clumsy mistakes that coincided with the rare times when he was holding a primed pen in hand. Warily, he pushed his chair towards it, bumping over sweaters and shirts lying on the floor in disarray. Lines defined themselves, and the subject no longer seemed to be a mere round spot. The teenager leaned forward for closer inspection. Bent lines protruded out on both sides, maintaining the symmetry of not one, but two circular shapes joined together like a snowman, the smaller one on top. The shape was about half an inch in length, including the crooked lines.

A spider.

He retracted his face, quick to put distance between himself and the predator. Was it poisonous? Maybe; he really didn't know a thing about spiders and the different species. The photos of those alien eyes and hairy fangs had always made his stomach churn, so he always flipped over the spider pages in his childhood animal encyclopedia.

But this one was no photo, and he couldn't just flip the page. It was real, and it was trespassing on his territory.

He had to kill it before it killed him. But with what? He gave his room a quick scan: the tissues were too thin to provide protection, he didn't want spider guts on his cell phone, his junior high graduation photo's picture frame was too precious to soil with blood, he certainly didn't want to ruin any of his clothes, he didn't want to touch blood-stained comic books if he ever felt like rereading them for the umpteenth time - nothing seemed to be a suitable match. Something thick enough to ensure safety but also something disposable, something he would never have to touch ever again - like a biology review book. He'd finished biology in freshman year, and he didn't plan on revisiting the subject. His little sister - well, she was smart enough to ace the class without the help of any review book, anyway.

Seizing the book with a hand on each of two corners, the young man turned back to the wall where he had located the trespasser - but that conspicuously new mark was no longer there. He surveyed the wall, expanding his search perimeter, but all he found were the same pen marks, the same ink smudges that had kept him company for years.

The spider had escaped.

The fear of seeing a spider doesn't quite measure up to the fear of not seeing a spider *after* seeing a spider. The air conditioning was suddenly too strong, and the cold froze the teenager in place. He was suddenly prey in his own home. His sanctuary from the outside elements was a sanctuary no more. It was now a battlefield.

He tiptoed over to the light switch next to the door and placed a finger underneath it. He flipped it, summoning a beacon of light from above. The light did little to change the room's illumination, as the sun's afternoon rays entered through the windows with ease, but the presence of all possible light eased an iota of the young man's anxiety.

His investigation began. First, a preliminary sweep of the room – nothing too in-depth, but enough to detect any extrinsic movement. Preferably, this simple step would be the last, but such was rarely the case when the predator had already escaped sight once, and this was no rare case. The only available option was to initiate a more meticulous search targeting specific likely hiding spots.

The first issue was the vast forest of T-shirts, socks, boxers, sweaters, sweatpants, shorts, and jackets that almost completely blanketed the entire floor. Certainly, the most ideal hiding spot would be a large area that provides a direct path to attack. His heart would not be set to rest until this security imperfection was remedied. But how to eradicate the obscurations without opening himself to enemy attacks? Well, that was what the review book was for. Perhaps its shape wasn't exactly perfect for the job – a bit wider than desired, and not quite as long – but it would effectively separate his hand from where the enemy might be lurking and at least delay an attack such that he would be able to drop the book should it be exploited as a bridge to his body. Applying the study tool as a broom, he swept the jungle away into his closet. If the assassin was hidden in the pile of clothes, then the young man would simply trap the enemy in the closet until it starved to death. While this would mean that the young man would lose access to the clothes other than those already on his person, such was a small price to pay to rid himself of his mortal enemy.

The deforestation was complete, but the target was still nowhere in sight. Either it got away or it was stuck in the closet. Best case scenario, it would be found soon, outside the closet, so that the teenager's fears would be put to rest now and not later. The search had to continue.

Next was the well-known habitat for monsters of all kinds: under the bed. Even in the summer afternoon it would be dark down where creatures dwell, so the teenager took a hand off his weapon to grab his phone and activate the flash. The teenager crouched down and lowered his head to look under, careful to keep his face a good inch off the wooden floor, and pointed his phone into the darkness. The searchlight first fell on a fuzzy clump of gray dust. No monster. A slight movement of the wrist, and the light revealed a lone sock, blanketed in more clumps of gray. Still no monster. Yet another turn of the wrist, and the young man spotted his DS on the far side of the bed, propped up against the heater. He was sure he had checked under the bed for the DS before, but it seems he had missed it. Still no monster. Just to be safe, the young man waved his light over the area once, twice, three times more, slowly scrutinizing every fleck of matter. Still no results. The enemy was too cunning to hide in a location strongly associated with its kind.

Before continuing with the investigation, the teenager decided he would retrieve the DS for the break after this incident was solved; such nerve-wracking effort surely earned him an hour or two of Mario Kart.

He brushed off the DS with his hand and placed it along with his phone on his dresser. Situated right beside his bed, where he was most vulnerable, the teenager recognized that the dresser was a strategic gem for his enemy and concluded that it must be inspected without delay. The front, six wide drawers organized in two columns of three, was clear; the white paint made it easy to spot anything that did not belong. On top of the dresser, however, was more complicated terrain. A line of cheap plastic participation trophies, painted gold to convince children that they were of some worth, stood, displaying the teenager's history in sports. Soccer, basketball, baseball, tennis – he had been actively involved in Little League and recreational teams back in elementary school, but after a few years of coaches putting him in games for the required ten minutes to please his parents before placing him on the bench again, he had shortly concluded that he lacked any athletic talent and quit all four sports by sixth grade. He was sure that he would feel better if he had never received the trophies at all – they incessantly reminded him that he never achieved anything more than bothering to sign up – but his parents had insisted that he keep them anyway, as "precious childhood memories" or something similar. To him, those memories were about as precious as the plastic those trophies were made of, but he never bothered himself to insist on throwing them away. In any case, the only thing hiding among the trophies was dust.

His generic bedside lamp, mostly used for late nights on the DS, sat on the edge of the dresser closest to the bed. The young man inched his head forward to look up the lampshade, and he accidentally brushed the lamp with his hair, scattering clouds of dust and sending him into a fit of sneezing. With every colossal sneeze, his head rampaged sporadically on the dresser, toppling his lamp, which luckily fell softly on the bed sheets, and clearing off an entire half of his dresser, irritating even larger swarms of gray powder. Firing like a machine gun for a full minute, the teenager's nose and mouth were quite sore and the floor a mess of trophies and a picture frame by the time the specks finally settled in their new homes.

How sly of his archenemy to lure him into a minefield. Our soldier had been careless, and now he faced staggering collateral damage. Before any further progress was made, rebuilding efforts were in order. One hand still holding the review book, he haphazardly set the participation trophies back on the dresser, which was easy enough considering how light they were. For the picture frame however, he was willing to lay down his arms and devote both hands to delivering it safely to its rightful place next to the lamp, propped up by the stand on its back and tilted at a forty-five degree angle toward the bed, the perfect position for visibility both from the bed and from off the bed.

The picture frame was a long wooden rectangle, several times larger than the typical picture frame to accommodate a particularly large photo. Depicted was a group of perhaps two hundred young students stuck frozen forever in the awkward phase of early puberty seated on rows of bleachers, a humongous mass of upper bodies smiling out of the picture frame. Not quite in the center, not quite near any of the edges, a slightly rounder version of the photo's owner stared out with a half-hearted attempt at a feeble smile on his face. However, that ghost of three years ago was not what the teenager, now momentarily distracted from the mortal game of hide-and-seek, first saw. Rather, his eyes strayed to the other side of the photo, where in the front sat a row of seven or so girls, all easily distinguishable by their matching gold-on-white shirts. In the middle sat a fairly tall young lady, her appearance that of a fairly standard pretty girl – shining golden hair, bright blue eyes, and a perfect smile neither too small nor too large. She looked more or less the same now, not having grown much since the end of eighth grade, when the photo was taken.

The girl, Sarah, was a fairly sociable girl – she enjoyed minor popularity but nothing too earth-shattering. She listened to a lot of hip-hop and pop music, her favorite movies were mostly romances and comedies, she wanted to become a veterinarian, her favorite subjects were English and math, she played the clarinet (second chair in the school concert band) – this was all information gleaned from short Facebook romps and bits and pieces of conversation our protagonist had overheard since Sarah's arrival to the school district in the seventh grade. She had assimilated seamlessly, and the young man now staring at the photo had admired her beaming smile and amicable personality ever since. He wondered what she would think if she saw him now – probably nothing, seeing how the longest conversation they had ever had together was four words long: "Hi," "Hi," "Bye," "Bye." Even should Hell itself freeze over and pigs learn how to sprout tremendously powerful wings and fly, there was no chance that the young man frantically searching for a spider in his room would ever become the lover of the girl who was most likely hanging out with her friends at the mall, and the young man was well aware, but even so he clung to his affections for the comfort they gave him when he looked at her picture or her clever Facebook statuses.

He had settled too long; it was about time for him to move on. The monster was still unfound, and there were still a few more stones unturned, namely his desk. He took the biology review book and continued.

The desk wasn't much more than a plane of wood balanced on two other wood boards painted over white. Shoved up against the corner, the desk used the wall to support part of the teenager's comic book collection – only part because the entire length of the desk was not enough to hold the dozens of graphic novels he owned. Those that could not fit were piled up next to the desk as if they had fallen off the edge. In front of the comic books were the flat computer monitor and the keyboard. The monitor, currently on screensaver mode, would be black as night and thus a possible camouflage area for the target, but luckily thin sprinkles of light dust had settled over the monitor the past couple years, and any spot of pure black would stick out as if it were in an undisturbed snow-covered field.

Underneath the desk, the most probable hideout, were only old binders whose rings had bent out of shape from years of physical abuse. Crowding two or three subjects' worth of handouts and looseleaf paper into a single inch-and-a-half-thick binder was not a long-term sustainable decision, but it meant fewer trips to the locker, which meant less dealing with the weird loud girl whose locker happened to be next to his.

The surface was the only place left. As previously mentioned, the monitor and keyboard were safe. A quick glance cleared the back of the monitor as well, and the comic books were pressed so tightly together that there were no gaps in between for any beast to crawl into. The only other object on the desk was the tissue box that sat to the left of the keyboard, but it was, like the monitor, all very lightly colored – the box a baby blue and the tissues white – so that no black creature would go undetected trying to hide there.

There was no spider.

Now just about the entire room had been surveyed, and the teenager had nothing to show for it. His enemy was still either on the loose or trapped in the closet with his clothes, but he was reluctant to surrender his right to spend time searching his room. There was no way he could focus on his work knowing that at any moment his life might be taken from him. And once he was positive his territory was safe, he would take some time to play Mario Kart to relax his nerves. By then it would probably be far past dinner time – a poke and a glance at his phone told him that it was now 5:47 – so he would eat to recover his strength. Then he would start working again, fresh and revitalized.

But first things first. He resumed his crusade to ease his own mind. The corners? Nothing. The windowsills? Just dust. The chair? Only loose threads that he mistook for spider webs until he realized spider webs aren't red.

Desperate, he double-checked the bed, the dresser, and the desk, but still he came out with nothing. Just when he was about to surrender and convince himself that the spider was in the closet, he remembered one detail that he had forgotten.

He had only checked one wall.

Of course, during his extensive investigations his eyes had happened upon the other walls every so often, and his eyes hadn't located anything amiss, but when you're not looking for something in a certain place, it's not too difficult to miss little details. For some odd reason he had glossed over the other walls as possible hiding spots, mostly because his walls were so white that any black creature would be plainly exposed to human eyes, but he did not consider that the spider might hide in plain sight. Perhaps he had underestimated the intellect of his nemesis in assuming an inability to comprehend mind trickery.

While he was at it, he might as well give the first wall another once-over, as some time had passed and the spider might have returned to the scene of the crime. That wall was the one that went along the length of his bed and the width of his desk. Other than those seventeen lines, there didn't seem to be anything outstanding in the field of white.

On the adjacent wall along the width of his bed hung a display of photos showcased in identical blue picture frames – obviously not his own handiwork, given the neat spacing. They even seemed to be arranged in chronological order; the pictures on the far left were noticeably fuzzy, as if there was a light drizzle of rain, while the pictures progressed in clarity as they were placed more to the right. Our investigator's eyes settled on the leftmost photo. In it a small boy, perhaps about nine or ten years old, was wrapping his arms around a smaller girl, who returned the affectionate gesture, in a field of grass. Both were displaying their fine rows of miniature teeth, giggling about some silent joke and blissfully ignorant of our investigator's life-or-death struggle. Distracted, allured by the pull of nostalgia, he took the time to examine each snapshot of simpler times. In the next, both children were much farther away, arms around each other's shoulders with the castle of Disney World standing grand and beautiful behind them. Then they were sitting next to each other at the dinner table with a square ice cream cake announcing "Happy 9th Birthday!" in blue frosting letters; the boy and the girl, who wore a paper crown two sizes too big, eyed the cake hungrily with greasy lips apart in silent but excited conversation, displaying bits of cheese stuck between their teeth. The timestamp at the bottom of the photo indicated that it was taken on August 20 of a year so old that it seemed foreign to the young man now. The next photo, the boy, traces of acne emerging on his face, was cross-legged on the carpeted floor, looking up from the Gameboy Advance in his hands. Then he was sitting on the couch next to the girl, both now clearly taller, their faces void of the roundness of childhood. His face was pulling up slightly at the corner of the mouth to please the camerawoman (their mother) as her face flashed a practiced, photogenic smile to skip over their mother's goading for a more cheerful memory to keep.

The nostalgia was fading away into remorse as the photos began hitting too close to home, so the young man pulled himself away and resumed his search, though his eyes were no longer quite so attentively wide open, his arms no longer poised to strike the spider at first sight. He merely glazed over the wall and saw no spider.

And he just stopped. His eyes subconsciously fixated themselves on that photo of an August 20 long ago, before she had begun flourishing in school, before his grades had started slipping, before she had grown into an attractive young woman, before he had found that puberty did not treat everyone equally, before she had pulled ahead of him, before he had relinquished himself of his responsibilities as an older brother because he believed he had fallen short of the title.

No longer motivated to pursue his enemy, the young man returned to his desk and looked at his blank paper – although it was no longer completely blank, as there was a small, black blot about half an inch long now decorating a line near the middle of the paper. The young man looked at the spider, then at the title of his essay assignment, then back at the spider again. The spider did not move, as if awaiting his response.

Deciding that it was about time he found his answer to the essay topic, the boy turned away from the spider and opened his door. He stepped out of his territory, took hold of the doorknob to his sister's room, and turned it.

"Shut Out"

"awesome. liked and favorited"
"love this arrangement."
"where can i get this???"
Keys clatter.
"dl link is in the video description."
Yet another ignorant mind rescued from the clutches of living blind. I lean back in my chair with my head upright, staring at my computer monitor. On the Bluetube page is the illustration of a happy blonde clad in a white apron over a black dress, pinning her black witch's hat on her head with a hand while flying high on her trusty broom over a

vast orange ocean. A vocal arrangement of the witch's theme song plays into my head via my black earphones. The song takes the original melody and puts it in a different key or something, giving it a lighter tone that I find very appealing. Of course, the vocalist's cute voice doesn't hurt, either; she sings somewhat cloud-like, if that makes any sense.

As I nod my head to the beat, I make an effort to examine the details of the illustration so my eyes aren't just wasting time. The lighting technique used with the sunset on the girl's form is pretty interesting, but I know nothing about CG, so I have no idea how the artist produced that kind of effect. I'm always telling myself to get into digital art some time, but it seems like such a hassle to learn. Besides, I have no means of getting my sketches onto my computer; with no scanner or graphics tablet, I only have the option of the mouse, and all attempts with the mouse have ended in some rugged mess. Well, it isn't like I'm good enough to make anything worthwhile even if I have the means to digitalize my stuff.

"Ruke! Ruke!"

Only my mom can mess up her own son's monosyllabic name.

"Ruke! Are you on the computer again?!" she shouts in Korean as she always does in the house. Even after living in America for some 20 years, my mom's ability to speak English is rather impaired. Not even English lessons on cassette could fix the heavy accent of a Korean-born woman.

I don't need to reply, but heavy footsteps coming down the stairs compel me to pause the video - and at such a good part! - and hastily minimize the web browser, leaving a random homework assignment from a couple months ago sitting on the screen. My mom'll see through the cover-up easily, but it's a habit that I still keep.

I swivel my chair eighty degrees and turn my head the remaining hundred to look at the ferocious figure of a furious Korean housewife storming her way hither in red slippers. Although I have no music on, I don't feel like plucking my earphones out of my ears, so I just leave them alone.

"You've been on the computer since the morning! Really, you should go outside more instead of watching your silly kids' videos all the time!" Just because they were illustrated doesn't mean that they were for children.

"I don't need to go outside, though..."

The presence of wrinkles on my mom's face is strong today. "Well, *I* need you to go outside! If you keep living like this, you'll grow up with no friends and you will die from a heart attack because you just look at computer lights all day!"

"Mom, I'm not going to get a heart attack."

Stubborn as ever, my mom thrusts her index finger at the front door behind her. "You go! Now!"

"And what am I supposed to do outside?"

"Go to the mall! Or eat! Do whatever normal kids do!"

The problem is that I don't *know* what normal kids do. Pretty much the only thing that I've gone outside for the past four years was church, and it's easy to avoid interaction in that large congregation. I have a private tutor for my schooling, so I don't even go to a public school. My life is pretty much spent inside the walls of my house, and I have no need to leave them yet.

My mom reaches into her pocket and pulls out, opens up, and sifts through her wallet before pulling out two twenty dollar bills. She holds them out to me, still angry. "Take these, and don't come back until you've used them!"

So here I am, left on the doorsteps of my own house, locked out with nothing but forty bucks and my cell phone in my pocket. And I'm *not* a runaway or homeless. At least, I hope I'm not homeless.

Well, I'm at a complete loss as to what to do. My map of the town is severely limited to the route that my parents take whenever we went to church. I know that if you go down the street from our little cul de sac and take a right, you will soon be greeted with another split. Going to the left, you go down a little and then you get to this four-way, where there is a doctor's office, a bar, a pizza place, and a convenience store. Take a right and you'll eventually reach the church that I go to every Sunday, but the distance on foot is enough to deter me from going to the one familiar place in the entire town. I walk into the convenience store.

As I open the door, the bell hanging from the top of it gives a cheerful ring that draws little more than a glance from the cashier. The aisles crowded with various goods ranging from potato chips to band-aids to cheap cell phone cases are almost intimidating to me; it has been several years since I last saw the inside of a store. I don't think that every single product gets enough sales to make it worth stocking up on, but maybe people just have a lot of money to spend, like my mom, who's *forcing* me to spend forty dollars.

I don't plan to spend all forty dollars in the convenience store, of course. I want to spend twenty-or-so dollars here, and then I'll go to the pizza place and buy a full-course meal. I'm not entirely sure how much that'll cost, but hopefully it'll empty my pockets.

Venturing aimlessly down an aisle, I notice another customer browsing the shelves. She looks like she could be around my age, but I can't really tell. I've seen very few Japanese and Chinese in person, but just from comparing the girl to the attendees of my primarily Korean American church, I'm pretty sure that she's Korean... probably. She's no model, but the customer is pretty enough for me to be sure that I would crash and burn if I tried to converse with her.

Well, this whole time I haven't noticed that I've been staring at this girl and she's noticed. Now I see that her head is up and her eyes are looking straight at me. At loss as to what to do next, I don't move. She looks down to the box that she's holding in her left hand and goes into some sort of flustered frenzy. Throwing me a glance that does not look pleased, she walks away with a bit of haste in her strides. With Medusa's gaze gone, I find myself able to move again. I put my hand to my heart and find it still beating rapidly. This is why I hated going outside.

Having restored my ability to function, I walk over to the row of stuff that the girl had been buying to satiate my curiosity and pick up a box. The box is blue and says something about a biodegradable applicator. In big white letters is the word "Tampaks." The word means nothing to me. What's a Tampak?

At this point, I remember that I had a job to do: spend forty dollars. I decide that I can start with this box, so I keep it. I don't care much about the functions of my purchases; I just want to get rid of my cash and go home. Throwing in a bag of chocolate chip cookies, a bottle of grape soda, a map, and some other things, I take my luggage to the counter. The cashier, a slim African-American man in a green apron, raises an eyebrow at my stuff, especially when his eyes fall on my box of Tampaks, but he doesn't seem to want to comment. I just stand in silence as he puts my purchases into a white plastic bag. It costs twenty-seven dollars including tax.

The bell cheerfully bids me farewell as I exit the very convenient store with a bulky bag in one hand and an open bottle of cold grape soda in the other. I stand in front of the door and fidget as I try to remember what I wanted to do. A stinging sip of carbonated drink jump-starts my memory, and I walk to the pizza place with a large sign with "HELLO MORNING" written in green, cursive letters. What a nonsense name for a pizza parlor. If not for the lit-up pizza pie on the store window, there would've been no way for me to know that it had anything to do with pizza.

To be honest, I'm a little disappointed when there is no bell that rings when I enter HELLO MORNING; the high-pitched notes could have helped take my attention away from the fact that there are only two other customers in the shop. Too few people make me feel like I'm more likely to be targeted for conversation.

At the counter is a corpulent, white man who towers over me with his hairy arms crossed and thick eyebrows dipped sternly. I do my best to focus on the fact that at least his moustache is smiling.

"What'll you be having?" The surprising gruffness of his voice, like one of a veteran sailor, makes me regret entering at all. What am I doing? I have enough food for a meal from the convenience store snacks! There's no point in coming to the pizza parlor, and now I'm going to soil myself in public and have to make an embarrassing trip all the way home. I shouldn't have come; I should've just thrown the remaining cash down the sewer or something. This was a horrible idea. Why did Mom have to do this to me? I could be at home, in front of the computer, watching more Bluetube videos, but instead I'm stuck in this humiliating situation with no way out.

They should have called this place "GOODBYE LIFE." Ha ha.

"Are you all right?"

I almost soil my pants for real; that man's voice is something fierce even when he's just asking an innocuous question. I must have spent a long time pitying myself, and this guy's probably getting impatient. I look down at the display of pizza underneath the counter and point at the first non-vegetable option I see. "Uh, that." I take care not to look up for fear of seeing a face that would fuel nightmares.

"The chicken breadcrumb pizza, then? Just one slice enough?"

"Uh, yeah." So much for buying a full-course meal.

A triangular spatula slides underneath a slice of my selection and takes it out of sight. I glance up, and thankfully, the man's back is turned to me as he places the slice in the metal oven behind him. He begins turning back towards me, so I look down again.

Wait, now what? I thought he would just give me the thing and I'd be on my way, but I guess that's not how it works? Am I supposed to be doing something, or do I just wait for the thing to bake? Should I stand here as I wait, or should I stand off to the side, or is that part of the counter over there supposed to be where I receive my pizza? Am I blocking the line or something? Oh good, there's no one behind me. But maybe I'm still supposed to stand off to the side, just in case someone comes? I dunno, maybe that's common courtesy or something. Is the pizza guy looking at my weirdly? I don't really want to look up, but maybe I'll get some clues as to what I should be doing. Nope, he's just talking to someone in the kitchen in the back of the store. That means that I'm not doing anything weird, right? I look at the other two customers, who seem to take no notice of my panic as they converse about something I can't hear. That almost definitely means that I'm fine, right? I look normal. There's no problem. Oh crap, the pizza guy's coming back. What's he- oh, he's just getting my pizza slice out. He's putting it on a paper plate, and he's coming back. I think this is almost over! Now he'll just tell me how much it costs and then-

"To stay or to go?"

So many questions!

"Uh, to... to go." Please just get me out of here.

The guy puts the pizza in a white bag while typing something into the cash register. "4.00" appears on the digital monitor. "That'll be four dollars," the guy says, a second too late for his words to be a surprise. I'd forgotten to get my cash ready, so I set down my bag of convenience store items and rummage in my pocket for what is probably the most agonizing five seconds of my life. I've only got three singles and one ten dollar bill, so I have to give him the ten. The cash register rings as it pops open, and the guy slaps my ten on top of a stack while simultaneously pulling out a five and a one in a single, deft movement. He's really quick with his hands.

"Here you go." The guy holds out the bills, and I, careful not to make contact with his fingers lest it tread on some uncharted social landmine, take my change and stuff them into my pocket.

He hands me the bag. "Yeah, thanks," I say with a shakier voice than I would have liked. I look up at him, and his face shows neither happiness nor anger, just a neutral tolerance. Being neutrally tolerated actually doesn't feel too bad.

I take the pizza bag and my convenience store bag in one hand and hold my grape soda in the other, and then I leave, though I don't really know where to go to eat the pizza. And I still have nine dollars left and nothing to spend it on. I don't need to go to the doctor's office, and I'm underage so I can't do anything in the bar. My options here are spent, it seems.

I look down a road I've been down before. There are trees, at least, so the shade will keep me cover from the sun. I don't really have anything to lose, I guess, so I start walking.

As murderous as the sun's rays can be, they do nice job lighting up the leaves overhead to produce a picturesque, glowing green. Then I realize that it's been years since I last had an overhead view from the road.

A few houses stand on the sides of the road. I walk by one I've seen a few times as we made the turn to go to church, a pale yellow house with a fence in the front. Now I see the pink bicycle leaning against the fence, white streamers falling from the end of each handlebar. Small cracks adorn the frame like battle scars, and I suppose they are essentially the same thing. A dirt-covered soccerball sits on the gravel, awaiting its next use. I notice swirls and stripes of dirt on top of the ball, where the kid probably trapped the ball with the bottom of his sneaker.

There's nothing particularly novel about the road. I've seen trees before, and I've seen houses on the sides of roads before, but when I'm walking so slowly rather than speeding by, the trees begin to look a little greener, the houses a little more alive.

Of course, it helps that I'm not running into any other people.

After a few minutes of aimless walking, I find a park. It's nothing fancy; a few wooden benches and an open metal wire trash can are lined up along one side, and there's a field of very green grass that leads to a small playground boxed off by long logs. The playground is just like the ones I used to play on all the time back in Moordale, with the pink slide that hurts if you put too much skin on it and the odd construction with floors that had diamond holes in them and the green monkey bars that are just high enough to be beyond my jumping reach (well, they used to be, at least; now I can probably reach them without fully extending my arm) and the swings that squeak a little bit when they move. Well, there's also this pink igloo thing that I've never seen before, but it looks like a nice place to make a hideout.

I sit down on a bench to take a break. As I open the pizza bag, which is spotted with grease stains by now, a fantastic aroma breaks out and sends my stomach into a grumbling fit, and only then do I notice how hungry I am. I take out the pizza on the plate and chomp off the tip of the slice, making sure to get a piece of chicken. The crisp breadcrumbs with the warm cheese and soft pizza bread and delectable chicken - perhaps it wouldn't be a terrible idea to visit HELLO MORNING again in the future.

Alternating between sips of soda and bites of pizza, I find myself full in less than five minutes. It turns out the slice was bigger than I thought, and I'm suddenly glad that I didn't buy a "full-course meal" of pizza.

But the problem remains: what do I do with my nine dollars? As far as I can tell, I won't be running into any more stores on this road, and I don't know if I'll have any better luck on the only other road left (besides the one that leads to church, which I know doesn't have any stores or anything). Maybe I should really just throw away what I've got left? But even though I spent twenty-seven dollars on random things in the convenience store, I'd feel a little bad throwing out money without buying anything at all. Should I just find a random person to give a surprise? As if I'd be able to just walk up to someone and give them something; I'd probably just end up humiliating myself. So then what do I-

"Excuse me."

I reel my head back in surprise at the close proximity of a voice, and I look up at a girl standing in front of me. Her jet black hair is all frazzled out and she's breathing a little heavily, but it's the girl from the convenience store, the girl I said was pretty enough for me to be sure that I would crash and burn if I tried to converse with her. Yeah, that one. She's talking to me for some reason, and she doesn't look happy.

"Oh, you're-" She seems just as surprised as I am at our second encounter, but unlike me, she's quick to recover. "Do you have a cell phone I can borrow by any chance? Mine just died and there's an important call I have to make."

"I, uh- yeah, I have one," I manage, still not quite sure what's going on.

For a moment, the girl stands there looking at me, and I refuse to move, petrified yet again. The weird arch in her right eyebrow seems to indicate that she's expecting something, but does she really want me to give her my cell phone? Is that normal? Maybe she saw how stupid I was before and thinks she can rob me or-

"Can I borrow your phone?" she asks, a little impatient.

"Uh, yeah." I fumble in my left pocket a little before I pull out my phone, a standard flip phone in its third year, and hold it out like the pizza guy held out my change. The girl, however, is not nearly as cautious as I was when she takes my phone with a quick "thanks" and flips it open with her thumb more skillfully than even I can. Her incredible thumb flies faster than my eyes can follow as she dials a number in a single, uninterrupted flurry of clicks. Is everyone in the real world so good with their fine motor skills?

The girl paces around in circles as she holds my phone to the side of her face, spreading germs that I might not mind so much as she mumbles something under her breath.

She suddenly stops in her tracks and lifts her head. "Alice?" To my surprise, her voice is, though urgent, more concerned than it is angry. "It's me, Sophia. Don't worry, don't worry; Mom and Dad aren't mad at you. It's gonna be all right, I promise. Where are you?" She begins pacing around again. "Wait, what? You're at school? You mean the elementary school? I just passed there; where are you at the elementary school? ...You're hiding behind the school? Okay, just stay put, all right? I'll be there in like two minutes. Mom promised to get pizza for lunch today." After a pause, she laughs, despite the apparent urgency of her situation. "Yeah, HELLO MORNING's. Yeah, you can get chicken breadcrumb pizza; you can get whatever you want. Just sit tight, okay? I'll see you in a little bit, Alice."

The girl, whose name I guess is Sophia, clicks a button on my phone to hang up. "Thanks," she says, moving back to me to hand me my phone back. But she stops herself and lifts a finger, telling me to wait a little, as

"Conformist"

"I don't get it."

Chulsoo, not even bothering to raise his hand, stares at me with the blankest of expressions. I return his stare while my mind checks and rechecks the current scenario.

"I just wrote it on the board," I say, tapping the whiteboard with my capped marker. On the board is the work to solve an algebra problem using a system of equations.

"Yeah, but I don't get it," he replies.

My patience with Chulsoo has always run thin, thanks to his school's odd curriculum of "Integrated Math" that has left him with spotty knowledge in mathematic territory the other eighth graders are already familiar with.

"You see, when you have two equations with like variables in problems like this one, you can add or subtract them to cross out y so you can solve for x. You need to get rid of all variables except for one."

"Kind of like Hitler," Daniel interjects.

Chulsoo glances in Daniel's direction before looking at me again. "But why does 2y – y become 0?"

"Because we multiplied the entire second equation by 2 on both sides so that the y's would cancel out."

"Oh. Okay, I get it now," Chulsoo says, but he says it in that vacant voice that makes it virtually impossible to judge whether he really gets it or just doesn't care anymore. I keep my eye on him for a second longer to gauge the truth behind his claim but ultimately decide to move on.

"Any other questions for this part?"

Daniel raises an arm as limp as his voice. "Yeah, what about number 8?"

"But you got that one right."

"Yeah, but I don't get it."

"You have all the correct work right there. I saw you write it."

Daniel stops in his tracks, recognizing his blunder. "Oh, you're right."

"Stop trying to waste time."

Daniel's mind is sharp, probably the sharpest in the class, but the ease with which he solves the problems we're currently going over affords him too much energy and concentration to direct into clowning around. It's frustrating because I know he's probably bored out of his mind, but he can't really move ahead of the class either. The capabilities of a single teacher are quite limited. Considering I have struggle with only four students, I can only imagine what it's like teaching twenty or so varied students in a single class.

"So does this mean there aren't any more questions?" I ask, feeling like an auctioneer refusing to accept a pitiful final bid. Considering that none of them got a perfect score, I'm pretty sure that there are some questions that should be asked but aren't getting asked.

"Bomin, how about you?" Usually I don't like calling students out like that, but he got a fifteen out of twenty, so I know that his grasp on solving algebraic equations isn't perfect.

Startled by the unexpected inquiry, Bomin glances at the other three students as if looking for a communal answer in their observing eyes. Finding nothing, Bomin adjusts his glasses, which were slipping from the rapid movements of his head, and replies with a nervous "No, no questions."

It's not like I don't understand his behavior – I've ignored my own questions in favor of moving the class along plenty of times before – and if he's like me, he probably thinks that it's better for the class as a whole to keep going without the interruption of his own questions; but now that I'm in the teacher's shoes, I realize how annoying it is to know that someone who should be asking questions refuses to do so. It doesn't really help to ignore gaps in knowledge that'll come back to bite you in the ass later. Nevertheless, I leave him be.

As for Ari, separated from the others by an empty chair as always, she was the only one to get a perfect score (Daniel made a stupid subtracting error on number 15), so asking her for questions would be a pointless endeavor. Nothing left to do but move on.

"All right, I guess we're all perfect at solving algebraic equations. Then let's go to word problems."

Pages shuffle as I wondered why the book separate word problems from everything else. Considering that word problems are just different representations of other units, why aren't they just distributed among their respective units based on content? Arbitrary compartmentalization can be puzzling at times.

The rustling of paper fades away by quarters until Chulsoo finally settles on page 507, and a momentary silence confirms that everyone is on the same page. Literally, at least.

I take a seat and plop my unwieldy Algebra I book on the end of the rectangular table. "All right, let's start with Example 1. Bill's jar contains only red, white, and blue marbles. The number of blue marbles is 4/5 the number of red marbles, and the number of red marbles is 3/4 the number of white ones. If there are 470 marbles in all, how many are blue?"

I look the problem over once more to go over the proper procedure in my head (define x as the number of white marbles, define 3/4x as the number of red marbles, define 3/5x as the number of blue marbles, add them all up to equal 470, solve for x, then solve for 3/5x). Then I look up. "Does anyone know how to start this?"

Only Daniel's hand rises, and with his eagerly inquisitive face, that hand can only be a declaration of war. But no one else's hands move, and now that they all see Daniel's flag raised, there is a significantly low probability of anyone making any moves in the near future.

"What is it, Daniel?"

Sometimes, it feels like the duty of a teacher is to step right on a known landmine just to get rid of it.

Daniel's hand descends, and he instead raises an incredulous tone. "Do they really think that they can promote patriotism by making us solve for the colors of this country's flag?"

Ari, Bomin, and Chulsoo stare at Daniel, speechless. Then they turn their heads to me, wondering how I'll respond.

I just shake my head in incredulity and wave my hand in the air as if to shoo the question out of my face. "That's not what you're supposed to be learning here."

But Daniel is unrelenting. "What you're teaching us is how to analyze and solve problems, right? The only reason this book gives word problems their own section is because we need to learn how to analyze paragraphs of text and context and pinpoint the mathematic problem hidden within. What I'm talking about is all about analyzing problems. According to my analysis of this math problem, it's a superficial attempt to foster nationalism among the youth of this country, and this reflects a societal problem in America. Society believes that repetitive exposure to 'American' things like the pledge of allegiance or the national anthem or the three colors of the American flag will somehow instill in American youth a sense of pride and love for our nation, but society underestimates us. Somehow, society fails to realize that the mindless repetition and obnoxious ubiquity of patriotic symbols only trivialize those symbols. Honestly, no one even actually says the pledge anymore, and I'm pretty sure we're all getting sick of seeing red, white, and blue marbles or beads or shirts or whatever in all our math problems. It's a shallow, transparent ploy on society's part, and it's only having the opposite effect."

Daniel stops and looks at me. All eyes that were focused on him, whether in admiration or in horror, are now again fixated on me.

Daniel's always been the most "Americanized" of the four students, both in actions and in words. He doesn't try to hide it, either (perhaps a component of what makes him so "American"). Upon first seeing him with his short hair and plaid polo shirts and jeans, it's not too hard to see that he's more American than he is Korean. He listens to American music, discusses American TV shows, and engages himself in football (the American kind, of course, not soccer); he's what some would call a "Twinkie" – "yellow on the outside, white on the inside." And the term is most fitting, seeing how Daniel consumes Twinkies, pizza, and coke for lunch every day while grimacing at the sight of Ari's usual rice, *kimchi*, and *duk-bok-ki*. On the very first day of class, when Ari opened her Tupperware container and the distinctly garlic smell of *kimchi* wafted out, Daniel covered his nose and commented with, to the word, "I don't know how you can stand eating rotten cabbage that's been spiced to death."

Even aside from his casual everyday interest, Daniel's ideals seem to rest with America as well. Certainly, he's in tune with the revolutionary principles on which this country was founded; I've had more than enough experience with his refusal to follow rules or his various ways of resisting the intended purpose of this class. Like I said, he has more than enough energy and focus to devote to his one-man rebellion. He holds himself with the self-assuredness of a typical American youth, too, refusing to bow to anyone, confident in his own ideas above those of others. Contrasting with traditional Korean culture, in which youth listen to their elders or subject their butt cheeks to the swinging side of a two-by-four, Daniel is adamantly anti-authority.

His parents probably had a hell of a time trying to raise him, considering that his parents are paramount examples of traditional Korean parents. From what they told me, they tried to get him into just about every Korean stereotype you can imagine – piano, violin, Tae Kwon Do, *hagwon* (Korean supplementary classes), you name it – and he didn't buy into a single one. At max, a week passed before he had his way and quit. It's hard to tell whether his parents were too lax in administering their authority and this resulted in the outspoken Daniel I see now or his parents were just as strict as other Korean parents and he was just exceptionally rebellious from the very beginning, but considering the typically assertive behavior of his parents, I'd be willing to bet on the latter.

I massage one hand with the other under the table. And now I have to stop the class and deal with this kid's aggression. I've always been terrible dealing with opposition.

"Or, you know, they could have just been looking for colors to use and said 'Hey, let's just use the colors on the flag because they're there,'" I reply, employing a voice shift in an attempt to lighten the tension. I get nothing.

At this point, Daniel is leaning forward and locking eyes with me, the tightening of his eyes nakedly exposing his disbelief. "You say that now, but just two hours ago you were telling us about how every little detail in writing is to be inspected and analyzed to our utmost capacity. 'The world is built on subtleties,' right? Why wouldn't that apply here?"

Why does he have to raise these kinds of questions? Is this class just some sort of place to kill time for him? Doesn't he realize that there are three other students in this class who can't afford to screw around the way he does, or that his parents are paying for these classes by the hour, or that society won't let you ask whatever questions you have whenever you want to?

I guess I haven't really gotten any better at this than I was in high school.

"Well, this isn't a critical reading book," I reply, hoping my voice is calmer than it sounds to my ears. "It's a math book." It's a sound argument in my head, but somehow I don't think it's going to cut it.

Daniel scoffs, and inside my head I sigh. It doesn't look like I'm going to win this battle. Hell, I've already lost, considering how much time we've spent so far on this tangent of all tangents.

"And that proves what?" Daniel retorts. "That's like saying, 'This is a history textbook, so of course it can't be propaganda.' Subtleties are everywhere, and they're *supposed to be subtle*, so it shouldn't be surprising if political propaganda pops up in a math book."

Something sounds off about his argument, but my mental hand-eye coordination is too slow, and I can't put my finger on it. I'm sure there's some logical fallacy or something somewhere in there, but I can't use it if I can't identify it. Maybe I should've taken more debate classes in college.

"Why don't we take a vote?" Daniel proposes with a voice too loud for the small room. "Who thinks that this book's color choice is just a coincidence?"

Silence. My heart sinks a little. The more I look like an idiot to these kids, the harder it's going to be to get them to listen to me.

Admirably showing no signs of smug victory, Daniel continues. "And who thinks that the red, white, and blue marbles are a stupid attempt at nationalistic propaganda?"

Silence. So they were just abstaining. My insides feel a few pounds lighter.

But Daniel is just irritated. "Oh, come on! There's no point to this if no one votes for anything!"

Praying for salvation, I slip my phone out of my pocket underneath the table and check the time. 12:40. Close enough to 1:00. "All right, it's time for lunch break now." I usually wouldn't stop in the middle of a problem, but at this point all I need is this "Get out of jail" card, and I'm not going to throw away a blessing from the heavens.

Daniel storms out alone, and after a few hesitating moments, Chulsoo and Bomin decide to leave together to buy their lunches.

Ari is the only one who always brings in her lunch from home, presumably because she prefers Korean food over the pizza and Chinese take-out that are near the building I'm teaching in. She reaches into her tote bag and pulls out her usual rectangular Tupperware box and unfastens the lid. Inside are circular cuts of *kimbap*, which is basically the Korean version of sushi rolls. The only real constant with *kimbap* is that there's dried seaweed on the outside and rice lining the inside of the seaweed; the stuff that's put in the middle can be pretty much anything, although Ari's uses fairly standard ingredients like egg, imitation crab meat, cucumber, and *bulgogi* (Korean barbecued beef). I've had variants with stuff like spam and sausage inside, though, so it can actually be made to fit more Americanized tongues.

I reach into my backpack and take out a peanut butter and jelly sandwich wrapped in a plastic bag. The most luxurious of all lunches.

The room is silent besides the rustling of the plastic wrap as I take it off. Even with Daniel gone, there's still some residual tension in the room. There is no clock in the room, but my mind imagines ticking anyway. Ari chews silently. I imagine I look like a feeble man after my poor show with Daniel. Well, I probably *am* a feeble man, but I can't let my students have that kind of image of me. I should at least try to salvage some of my respectability as her teacher and senior.

"So, Ari, you go to a private school, right?"

She seems a little startled by my inquiry and looks up at me through her thin-rimmed glasses. "Yes," she almost whispers, her slight accent leaking through a little in that single syllable.

"How do you like it?" I ask before taking a bite out of my sandwich.

A thought flickers across Ari's face, but she normalizes it and replies with a generic, safe "it is okay" before looking down at her fascinating Tupperware and taking another *kimbap*.

In a lot of ways, Ari is the polar opposite of Daniel. She shies away from his American tastes in favor of the Korean culture she was raised in until a few years ago — well, at least from what I can tell from her Korean lunches, Hello Kitty cell phone strap, and her parents. Really, most of what I know about Ari comes from her parents, who strike me as fairly generically Korean in their parenting. The first day they came to meet me to see who I was and whether they thought I would suffice for their needs, Ari's parents pretty much told me Ari's life story, recounting how she started learning piano at five years old and has been at the top of her class all throughout elementary school and middle school and has been awarded for her paintings as early as fourth grade and on and on. I didn't really retain most of that conversation, to be honest, but I got a general sense of what was going on. Unlike Daniel, who adamantly rebelled against the hand of authority, Ari fell under the will of her parents and allowed them to determine the course of her life. I don't know if growing up in Korea had anything to do with Ari's passive growth, but her parents certainly fostered (or drilled) a sense of filial piety in her. And not just filial piety, either; she bends to the will of any authority, even that of her peers, like when Chulsoo asked her if she wanted to get pizza with him, and she said yes, even though the reluctance was pretty clear on her face. Just to avoid disrupting the state of her environment, she'll do anything.

But sometimes, bending to the will of others is a good thing. Without parents goading them to tackle new challenges or try new things despite the fear and discomfort, a lot of people would never grow out of childhood, or at least they would take much longer to mature. And the views of outside persons sometimes offer more truth than one's own view, and the opinions of others are sometimes worth keeping over one's own. There are times when I regret quitting the piano in middle school, because proficiency in playing music can be used for so many things, and I see my friends having *fun* playing piano and actually *wanting* to practice. But back in middle school, I never would have believed that playing piano would ever be considered "fun," and I got fed up, and I quit. If my parents hadn't allowed me to quit, I probably wouldn't have thanked them, but maybe I'd be a little better off.

And the more obvious benefit of conformity is that things get to run smoothly. I get to teach math in my math class rather than get sidetracked into some unnecessary political argument, and I don't get interrupted by a question every minute.

So is it good to submit to others? Is it good to conform? But for all Daniel's faults, I can't deny that in some ways, I admire his self-confident stubbornness. He knows exactly what he believes and why he believes it, and he won't be shaken from his positions. What's it like to be so sure about what you believe and what you want, regardless of how society or authorities or peers tell you to live? Maybe a little rebellion is good, too.

Conformity reduces individuality but takes advantage of the wisdom of others and allows communities to run smoothly. Nonconformity promotes one's own personal direction but jams up the cogs of society.

So where do we draw the line?

"Fiction"

I am a fictional character.

The thought jumps out in my mind suddenly, like a forgotten appointment. As if someone planted it in my mind, this thought I innately know to be truth just as I innately know that murder is evil. It is true, truer than the laws of physics, truer than the cold air conditioning and the taste of my breath and the white of my ceiling and the softness of my bed.

I am a fictional character. This means that I live in a fictional world. This means that I live with fictional people, interact with fictional objects, go to fictional places, dream fictional dreams. My mother, father, and sister are all lies.

My house is a lie; my school is a lie. Everything I know is nothing but the creation of some person sitting at a desk, coming up with my newest conflict or my latest success. Someone who has the power to control everything that has to do with me.

I sit up - and pause. That too was determined by someone else. My muscles did not make me sit up; someone writing words made me sit up. A chilling thought. An overwhelming, imprisoning thought. I try to ignore it - after all, there is nothing I can do about it, for I am nothing but a character in someone's story.

I toss aside the common application packet I had been staring at. Suddenly, selecting colleges doesn't seem so important anymore.

I follow the packet with my eyes as it lands in a disordered heap on my desk. The desk that stands at the foot of my bed, my initials scratched out of its white paint, right beside a messy "KH," the initials of my third grade crush - that desk with its ancient memories only exists because someone wrote it so. And my cheap gold-painted trophies in soccer, baseball, basketball - mere participation trophies, but trophies nonetheless - are only real because someone described them with strokes on a keyboard.

I try standing up off my bed, but my legs fail underneath me and I stumble. The whole world seems to quake loosely, as if anything at any moment might just fall out of place. Someone made my legs falter. Someone made me fall. Someone made my knee smash into the wooden floor and shake the house. Fuck you.

I get up on my feet, gingerly touching my bruised knee. Even if the pain is fictional, it's still pain.

Enough of this.

The stairs feel flimsy beneath my feet, as if they

might fall away at any moment, like those donut-shaped blocks from *Mario*. Wait, *Mario*'s fictional, right? Is it fiction within fiction, or is it perhaps something from "reality," imported into my world? How much of my world works the same way as the "real world"? Maybe things that exist in my world, like touchscreen phones and laser surgery, are simply ideas created by the author? Maybe the author lives in a primitive world of carriages and old-fashioned top hats? I could be living in someone's sci-fi imagination.

But why would I exist in a sci-fi story? There is nothing exceptional about me; I'm not a secret agent on a mission to topple a dystopian society, and I'm not a scientist involved in the latest breakthrough of time travel technology. No matter how I look at it, any sci-fi narrative centered around me would be heart-breakingly boring. And if I'm to be one of those normal citizens who gets caught up in a vast plot determining the fate of human society, that's ruined because I now know that I live in a fictional world. Why would the author give me the knowledge that I live in a fictional world? Is this some sort of experiment? Am I some damn test subject being observed for unusual behavior? But the author is the one who determines my behavior, so wouldn't that be pointless? Why do I know this? Does everyone know this? Have I been out of the loop all this time? Or am I some sort of "Chosen One" whom the author has decided to give exclusive knowledge of how fake this world is?

Seriously, enough of this! This isn't helping!

My sister is in the kitchen, seated at the dinner table with a bowl in front of her. A laptop next to the bowl is angled in her direction, but she seems to be ignoring it completely. She's drawing a whirlpool with a metal spoon in the milk, sending Frosted Flakes into a mindless swirl, revolving around the the center of the bowl. She glances up at the sound of my footsteps before returning her vacant attention to her cereal.

I stop. I watch her raise her spoon with a catch of a few flakes and some milk. I imagine her body framed by green lines, the polygons of her skin shifting to her movements. Like a computer-generated model. Artificial.

The sight makes me sick so I do my best to turn off my imagination.

"You alright?"

I notice that my thumb is pressed against my skull, the veins along my wrist popping out of my skin like pipelines. Grace, swirling her Frosted Flakes again, looks at me curiously. Her eyes look so real, so alive even in their confusion - but they're just-

"Hey, Josh!" Josh? Who gave me that name? My parents, or someone else? Who gave me that name? Who named me? Who made me? Who-

A cold smack to the cheek. Gentle, but firm. My thoughts are suddenly gone.

A wet spoon. Two large, dark irises. The outline of a face - my face - in two pools of bold brown. Grace's eyes, right in front of me. They're there. She's there. Grace is here. In front of me.

My face resists, but I manage to lift the corners of my lips in what I hope is a reassuring smile. "Sorry. I'm all right." Of course I'm not, but I had to say something.

Grace is not convinced. "You on something? You look anything but all right. If you think you're going nuts, tell me before you do anything stupid, okay?"

Goddammit, why did my author have to give me a "caring older sister" type? Do I reject her, a creation of imagination? Do I spurn her, the most painful reminder of how even those closest to me in this world of mine are, at the end of the day, someone's words? Do I despise her for always seeming to care in her own way when in fact those emotions are injected into her by some "higher being"? Do I-

Another cold smack, but this time harder. "You need to get yourself together." Her dipping eyebrows and no-nonsense gaze remind me of when Mom caught me moping about a math research paper and spurred me into action with a few commanding words. Are all women such strong disciplinarians? Or maybe that's just in my world? Maybe that's how my author views the "fairer sex"? Is my author a guy or a girl, anyw-

The cheek again, but this time it's a warm touch. Grace's hands cup the sides of my face as if she's trying to make sure I don't try to look away; she hasn't done this since elementary school. Her brown eyes, gentle but troubled, try to look through my eyes into my head. I can't help but consider how out of character this is for her, how odd that after the recent years of being a casual, cool sister, she suddenly begins getting so worked up over me, as if she knows what I'm going through right now. Is this my author trying to pacify me with a warm gesture? Is he (she?) trying to use Grace to tame me as you would tame a wild dog with a slab of raw meat? Fuck that's a disgusting analogy, I shouldn't have thought of it.

"Josh." I blink, savoring the night, and meet her gaze. Her hands are warm. "Josh," she repeats, "are you all right?" It's a typical, cookie-cutter question, but each word is heavy with thought.

I don't know how to respond. For a moment I actually consider telling her that she's a lie, that I'm a lie, that Dad's a lie and Mom's a lie, that we're all bound in a world of words typed on a screen, but there's no way that she'll believe me and there's no way I can come up with a line that even I'll believe, and then she'll just think I'm crazy and I'll think I'm crazy and we'll have to suffer even though this is just a fictional world and it's not real, we'll still have to suffer because of some asshole playing God over my tiny, insignificant, worthless, fake, pathetic excuse of a-

"Josh." Her voice is resolute as she gives my brain a small quake to re-center my eyes on hers, and only then do I notice that my eyes had been sneaking off to the side. Her gaze demands an answer. Normally the only right answer to that question is "Yeah, I'm fine," but it seems wrong to use a stock answer when Grace is behaving in such an earnest manner. On the other hand, maybe that's all the more reason not to tell her the truth. Whether some asshole wrote it this way or not, she's still my sister and she'll still worry over me if I tell her about all my problems and-

"Josh."

"N...no." The single syllable feels foreign, as if I'm saying it for the first time. I'm not sure exactly what I've done, but I couldn't help it. Maybe it was Grace, maybe it was the author, I don't really know, but before I knew it I had already started, and once I start with that "n" the rest of the word just defines itself and there's nothing I can do to-

"Let's go."

It takes my mind a moment to process even the simplest of stimuli. "Wait, what?"

"There's a movie I want to watch," Grace says, and with that, she walks past me and trots up the stairs.

Motionless, I listen to her footsteps fade away with each thud. The thought of watching a fictional movie doesn't really sit well with my current state of mind, but maybe I'd be able to immerse myself in the movie and forget about everything else? I suppose it's possible that the overwhelming, nonstop stimulus of a good movie might overpower my thoughts.

Jangling keys announced Grace's return to the first floor. She stops on the second-to-last step to turn to me from higher ground. "You ready?"

"...Sure." At the very least, the movie should serve as a better distraction than my soon-to-be-empty house. Hah, maybe it'll even be a clue from my author, a key to my solving the mysteries of my existence, a movie with a moral that'll tell me some inspiring message about how to deal with being a figment of someone else's imagination. Wouldn't that be just grand?

Assuming that my author didn't write out the entire sequence of the movie and my watching it, I think I can actually experience things without my author writing about them. Maybe it's because it was implied in an earlier scene. Do I have freedom during these segments of time skipping? Well, probably not, not as long as my author gets to write the scenario afterwards. He (she?) still has the power to decide the outcome, after all. As long as my author keeps writing, I will be confined to his (her?) words.

But then again, every story has an ending. When my story ends, will I be free? Or will I cease to exist? Maybe my author will write my story up until my death after a time skip. Or... my death might be soon. Assuming I'm the protagonist (an arrogant assumption, maybe, but I only know my own story), then after I die, will my whole world end? Back when there was all that commotion about the supposed "end of the world," my English teacher talked to the class about how people aren't wired to fully grasp the reality of how even after they die, the whole world will go on as if nothing happened. That was her explanation for why people keep coming up with more or less baseless theories about when the world's going to succumb to fire and flood, but if I truly am the protagonist, then I might not need to worry about that. Or maybe the end of the world is nearer than I think. Well, that might be a bit of a stretch; it's not like all fictional stories end with the apocalypse. Or maybe that's just what we think? Maybe the apocalypse isn't actually about fire and floods and earthquakes ravaging the planet - maybe it's just a sudden... end. There's an odd thought. Truman figures out that his life is a television show, Meryl is taken away, Truman sails off on the *Santa Maria*, he enters the real world, and then the world ends. Is that how it works? Once my story ends, will the world end?

Or maybe I'm actually a supporting character, not the main character. But if I'm just a supporting character, would my thoughts exist in such vivid detail? If I'm a supporting character, the author is either delving very deep into a side character's head, or there are things in this world that can exist outside of what the author writes. If the latter is the case, then the end of the story would not mean the end of the world; I'd be free.

But what difference would that make? I dunno, maybe it wouldn't really be that different after all. For all I know, I could be "free" right now and not even know it. Hopefully I'll feel some noticeable change when the written story ends.

I suppose there are a lot of possibilities, but I'm likely not going to get the answer just by sitting on this toilet. Maybe the author will give me another epiphany out of thin air, but he might not, and I don't want to be waiting around for dozens of subplots to get wrapped up before I can figure this all out. Hopefully this is a short story and not a drawn-out series.

Anyway, Grace is probably waiting on me, and this toilet seat isn't exactly comfortable, so I get up and leave the bathroom to return to our table.

As soon as I open the door, the murmuring of the people in one of the mall's many small but crowded fast food restaurants hits me as if I just jumped my head's volume setting from fifty percent to a hundred. Friday nights of the summer are, after all, the rush hours of mall business.

Grace is seated in a chair across a small, square table from an empty spot on an inner, cushioned bench that stretches along several other square tables, all the others already occupied. Next to my burger, her smoothie is untouched. So she was waiting.

I slide into the cushioned bench. "Sorry to keep you waiting."

She smirks. "I was about to go to CVS to get you some laxatives, but I guess you managed to pull through. You make me proud."

"I'm sure I do, though I don't want to be reminded of my bathroom adventures while we're eating." But really, I'm glad that she's acting normally after her atypical silence during the car ride and after the movie.

I take my "classic" burger and peel the cheap paper off it like onion layers. The reward for my efforts is a pencil-thin cut of questionable beef, a papery leaf of lettuce, a mushy slice of tomato, and two flimsy pieces of bread that look more like wet cardboard than buns. Generic food for a generic guy, but it's been paid for by said generic guy's sister, so I don't really have a right to complain.

I take a bite. It's all right, I guess.

"Hey Josh," Grace starts, her returning smirk a clear sign that what's to follow will not be fun for me, "now that I think about it, I haven't really asked you about what's happened with you and Priscilla since Christmas. Any luck on that front?"

"Not really. We talked a few times in English class and I saw her once here. With her boyfriend." That doesn't really matter, though, since Priscilla's fictional, too. She's as fake as my infatuation with her.

"She got a boyfriend? Well, that sucks. What's he like?"

"I dunno, I've only seen him a few times. He seems all right, though, and Priscilla seems happy enough, anyway – at least, from what I can tell."

"Most people 'seem all right,' but it's what's behind the seeming that you need to check."

"I'm not gonna start spying on them, if that's what you're suggesting."

"I'm not saying that, but just keep in mind your chances aren't totally shot. You might still be the right guy for her." Well, if I'm a protagonist, I guess that'd help my chances as long as this doesn't boil down to one of those things where the protagonist learns that his affections were stupid anyway and moves on. Or this becomes a revenge story about me going around killing people out of jealousy. Although, if I do kill people out of jealousy, would that really be my fault? After all, I have no choice but to do as my author writes.

Grace gives me a funny look. Maybe I had a suspiciously pensive expression on my face. "That doesn't mean barge into their relationship and take her, just so you know. Sometimes you just need to wait a little." So no killing people out of jealousy.

"Yeah, it's not like I'm really pining for a relationship right now, anyway. I'm fine as it is."

I hear a trace of distraction in Grace's laugh, as if her mind is elsewhere. "You're probably right on that one." She raises her strawberry mango smoothie in one hand and takes a sip from the straw, and suddenly, she's the one with a pensive expression.

I watch her for a little bit, but she shows no signs of surfacing. "And how's college for you?" I ask. It seems that interrupting silent thoughts is what we're doing here, so I figure I should contribute.

Grace's eyebrows shoot up as she looks up from her smoothie, apparently surprised that I took the initiative to say something, before she settles into a neutral expression. "Well, I guess it was all right. Finals were tough and I had to study pretty much whenever I had free time, but second semester wasn't too bad. The people there are really fun, too."

"Fun, huh." I pause and hesitate, but I've already surprised myself with my honesty in admitting my unsound condition to Grace, so speaking my mind isn't so difficult at this point. "You don't regret your decision?"

Nodding to herself with a small smile on her face, Grace takes another sip. "It's not like I know what it's like to live a student of another college, but no, I can't say that I regret ending up where I am now." She leans back in her chair and stretches her arms up in the air. "How's thinking about college going for you?"

I should've known my direction of inquiry would have led to this, but it's too late to regret it now. Or maybe this is what I actually wanted. Or what my author wanted. "It's... not really going."

I'm met with a mix of amusement and admonishment. "I know it's summer and all, but you're going to be a senior before you know it, and trust me on this: you don't want to be doing college apps during school. Schoolwork just makes it too easy to push applications back and back and back until you have to pull all-nighters to complete them."

"Well, I haven't even decided which colleges to apply to yet, so I've got a way to go before starting to complete applications."

"You still haven't got any idea of where you want to go?"

"Not really. I mean, no one talks about any colleges other than elite schools that I can't get into. There's a clusterfuck of colleges out there, and I'm just one guy. How am I supposed to know where to apply to?" Even though I know it doesn't *really* matter, even though I know that even the colleges are fictional and that the jobs that they'll lead me to will be fictional, my author insists that I still care.

"Yeah; that's why you have to take matters into your own hands. You have to research a little bit on your own."

Before I even know it, my mouth runs off on its own. "You know how bad I am at 'taking matters into my own hands.' I don't even have the balls to handle a relationship, so of course when it comes time to choose one path out of hundreds for my life, I freeze up and do nothing. It's been this way ever since I was born. That's why I just dropped out of every single sport I ever tried – because when people started actually giving a damn about skill, when people stopped giving out participation trophies, I couldn't make the decision to try! I swear, even if I discovered that I could save the world from some supreme overlord who's controlling everyone's minds, I wouldn't be able to make the decision to do even *that*." Even as I speak, I mentally slap myself for saying too much.

Suddenly the surrounding murmur of the restaurant seems quiet, and I realize I was getting carried away with my rant, and my voice might have escalated more than intended. Few heads actually turn, but I still divert my gaze downward at my crumpled burger wrapper until Grace's voice reaches me.

"Josh. Look up at me."

I look up, and I feel a pang of relief when I see a gentle smile rather than a disapproving glare. My author is really spoiling me.

"Well, first of all, it's because not everyone can stand up to evil overlords that college guides and counselors exist," Grace says. Although I refuse to show it, I'm a little comforted by the fact that she finds my insecurities light enough to joke about; at least that means they don't indicate clinical insanity. Though juvenile angst might really be just as bad.

Grace takes a sip before continuing, now adopting a sterner tone. "And second of all – well, making decisions is a curious process because everything we do is a decision on one level or another. If you want to make things complicated, you could even say that for every decision we make, we make a decision to make that decision. Or we make a decision to make a decision to make a decision. Basically, what I'm trying to say is that no one is born making big decisions; first, they make the decision to make decisions."

Her serious gaze melts into a reassuring smile. "Get it? Decisions start somewhere, and *you* decide when they start. No one else does. You do."

At the end of the day, I'm back where I started: lying on my bed, staring at the ceiling, only the moon is up instead of the sun. But now I can see why people spill out their emotions to other people all the time; whether it's knowing that someone else has heard my feelings or it's simply verbalizing them, talking to Grace somehow helped.

But while it was nice not having to think about my reality, I don't think I can sleep until I salvage something out of this mess.

As long as my author writes, he can determine whatever happens to me or in me. If he stops - well, I still don't really know what'll happen if he stops. The two possibilities, I think, are that either my world will cease to exist, or it will exist apart from the author. And if it exists apart from the author, then my world and everyone in it, including me, will no longer be fictional, and we will become autonomous beings.

And if my world ceases to exist when the story ends, then there's no hope for my world's autonomy after all, and then there's really nothing I can do about it, so for now I'll just assume that when the story stops, my world is freed.

The only possible solution, other than changing the laws of the universe and reality, is to have the story end. This story needs to end.

The question is, how does the story end? If you consider how stories typically end, usually there's some sort of resolved conflict or suggestion of future hope or a suggestion of future despair or death or - really, it could be anything.

Death. If I die, will the story end? If I really am the protagonist, perhaps. Or the author could just switch over to another character, but that usually doesn't happen all that often. Though I know I'm no protagonist material, supposing that I *am* the protagonist, if I died, perhaps, maybe my world would be free.

Free? From what? There is joy, there is despair, there are triumphs, there are tragedies – my world is already pretty full of stuff. And maybe the author will not be an idiot and make good decisions.

I sit up and locate on my desk the messy pile of papers that supposedly determines the rest of my life. Who knows, maybe the author'll let me get into Harvard for all the crap he's given me.

And then what? I'll go to a Harvard imagined by my author, I'll receive an education from my author, I'll make friends created by my author, I'll get a job chosen by my author, I'll get married to a girl conceived by my author, I'll die in a ditch dug out by my author. I will never have to make a decision on my own ever again. No risk of failure, no responsibility for mistakes – in a way, it's the most carefree lifestyle possible. If I were ignorant of my world's fictitiousness, I probably would have loved the idea of such a sinecure, but knowing that someone is sitting a desk, typing up my destiny, makes my reality primitively clear.

I want to write my own life.